Advance Praise for *The Conscript*

"*The Conscript* gives the Tigrinya novel its early framing contour, as it shows sophistication and maturity in the depiction of the inner turmoil and real-life characteristics of its characters. It is a novel that grapples with issues of identity, self-agency, war, and the traumatic effects of (de)colonization on the human psyche. Read it and see for yourself how canonical novels like *Things Fall Apart, Weep Not, Child, Houseboy, The Bluest Eye,* among others, are eerily prefigured in an early African-language novel."

—Ali Jimale Ahmed, Professor and Chair, Department of Comparative Literature, Queens College, CUNY

"*The Conscript* is a harrowing journey into the experiences of an Eritrean man who, after being recruited into the Italian army, is forced to fight in its war to subjugate Libyans. This is a novel of great irony and power. Its translation into English is a gift to American readers."

—Laila Lalami, author of *Hope and Other Dangerous Pursuits* (2005) and *Secret Son* (2009)

"Gebreyesus Hailu does Africa great service in recounting an all but forgotten and therefore all the more reprehensible chapter in African colonial history. In the same spirit, Ghirmai Negash's superb translation brings back to world literature an Eritrean literary jewel of global and timeless relevance."

—Alemseged Tesfai, author of *Two Weeks in the Trenches* (2002)

The Conscript

This series brings the best African writing to an international audience. These groundbreaking novels, memoirs, and other literary works showcase the most talented writers of the African continent. The series will also feature works of significant historical and literary value translated into English for the first time. Moderately priced, the books chosen for the series are well crafted, original, and ideally suited for African studies classes, world literature classes, or any reader looking for compelling voices of diverse African perspectives.

Welcome to Our Hillbrow: A Novel of Postapartheid South Africa
Phaswane Mpe
ISBN: 978-0-8214-1962-5

Dog Eat Dog: A Novel
Niq Mhlongo
ISBN: 978-0-8214-1994-6

After Tears: A Novel
Niq Mhlongo
ISBN: 978-0-8214-1984-7

From Sleep Unbound
Andrée Chedid
ISBN: 978-0-8040-0837-2

On Black Sisters Street: A Novel
Chika Unigwe
ISBN: 978-0-8214-1992-2

Paper Sons and Daughters: Growing Up Chinese in South Africa
Ufrieda Ho
ISBN: 978-0-8214-2020-1

The Conscript: A Novel of Libya's Anticolonial War
Gebreyesus Hailu, translated by Ghirmai Negash
ISBN: 978-0-8214-2023-2

THE CONSCRIPT

A NOVEL OF LIBYA'S ANTICOLONIAL WAR

by

GEBREYESUS HAILU

Translated from the Tigrinya

by

Ghirmai Negash

Introduction by Laura Chrisman

OHIO UNIVERSITY PRESS • ATHENS

First Edition (in Tigrinya)
Pietro Silla Printing Press, Asmara
([1927], 1950)

Ohio University Press, Athens, Ohio 45701
ohioswallow.com

Printed in the United States of America
Ohio University Press books are printed on acid-free paper ∞ ™

20 19 18 17 16 15 14 13 5 4 3 2 1

Cover image: Illustration from *L'Illustrazione Italiana* of General Baratieri landing at Massua in 1885

Library of Congress Cataloging-in-Publication Data
Hailu, Gebreyesus, 1906–1993.
The conscript : a novel of Libya's anticolonial war / by Gebreyesus Hailu ; translated from the Tigrinya by Ghirmai Negash ; introduction by Laura Chrisman.
p. cm.—(Modern African writing)
"First edition (in Tigrinya), Pietro Silla Printing Press, Asmara ([1927], 1950)."
Includes bibliographical references.
ISBN 978-0-8214-2023-2 (pb : alk. paper)—ISBN 978-0-8214-4445-0 (electronic)
1. Italy—Colonies—Africa—History, Military—Fiction. 2. Libya—History—1912–1951—Fiction. 3. Eritreans—Libya—Fiction. 4. Draftees—Eritrea—Fiction. I. Negash, Ghirmai. II. Chrisman, Laura. III. Title. IV. Series: Modern African writing.
PJ9111.9.H35C6613 2012
892.833—dc23

2012040505

Contents

Translator's Note

This is the first complete translation of *The Conscript* into English or any other language. Since 1995, when I first read the novel, I have had a strong desire to translate it as a tribute to celebrate the vitality of African-language literature(s). More than a celebratory gesture, however, my decision to make the novel available in translation was inspired by my wish to share this extraordinary story of human suffering and moral courage with my family members, friends, and colleagues in African and world literature studies, who encouraged me on several occasions to translate the book.

The Conscript is a magnificently complex novel both in its thematic concerns and in its form. Equally fascinating is the life of its author, Gebreyesus Hailu, who was born in a small village in Eritrea in the early twentieth century and who rose to become a prominent literary and public voice. This is not the place to enter into a long discussion of the book or to provide an extended biography of the novelist. I will content myself here with offering a few remarks about the themes and language of the novel; a brief profile of its author; some reflections about how the novel, set on the boundary of modernity and tradition, both engages with and revisits ritualized oral versions of the history of conscription in Eritrea; and my own engagement with the text as a translator. My hope is that the information provided will enhance the reader's appreciation of the novel. I begin by offering a short description of the author.

Gebreyesus Hailu was born in 1906 in Afelba, in the southern region of Eritrea.[1] At an early age he learned to read and write. He attended San Michele School in Segeneyti and in 1923 began his education at the Catholic Seminary of Keren. In 1924, he began his studies at the Ethiopian College in the Vatican, where he earned his *licenza ginnasiale* in 1927, finishing the program in three years rather than in the standard five. Hailu proceeded to earn advanced degrees in philosophy and theology, and in 1937 obtained his doctoral degree in theology, writing his dissertation in Latin. On his return to Eritrea, Hailu became an influential figure in the cultural and intellectual life of Eritrea during the Italian colonial period, and in both Eritrea and Ethiopia in the post-Italian era. He was the vicar general of the Catholic Church in Eritrea and played several important roles in the Ethiopian government—including cultural attaché at the Ethiopian Embassy in Rome, member of the national academy of language, and advisor to the Ministry of Information of the Ethiopian government—until his retirement in 1974. He died in 1993.

Acclaimed by its Eritrean readers as eloquent and thought provoking, this classic Tigrinya novel by Hailu was written in 1927 and published in 1950. Although fiction and nonfiction prose in the Eritrean language predate it, *The Conscript* is the first novel in the literary history of Eritrea and one of the earliest novels written in an African language. The book depicts, with irony and controlled anger, the staggering experiences of the Eritrean *ascari,* soldiers conscripted by the Italian colonial army to fight in Libya against the nationalist Libyan forces fighting for their freedom from Italy's colonial rule. As Laura Chrisman insightfully notes in her introduction to this edition, Hailu, anticipating such midcentury thinkers as Frantz Fanon and Aimé Césaire, paints a devastating portrait of Italian colonialism. Some of the most poignant passages of the novel involve the awakening of the novel's hero to his ironic predicament of being both under colonial rule and the instrument of suppressing the colonized Libyans.

The novel's expressive language is just as distinct as its thematic quality. Particularly moving are the descriptions of Libya. Those passages awe the reader with mesmerizing images, both disturbing and tender, of the Libyan landscape, with its vast desert sands, oases, horsemen, foot soldiers, and wartime brutalities. (As the reader will find, it is uncanny how these images connect with the satellite images that were brought to the homes of millions of viewers around the globe in 2011, during the country's uprising against its former leader, Colonel Gaddafi.)

A further essential aspect of the novel's interest is its engagement with oral tradition. As Harold Scheub once noted, reflecting the conclusion of many Africanist scholars, "There is an unbroken continuity in African verbal art, from interacting oral genres to such literary productions as the novel and poetry."[2] In *The Conscript,* this "unbroken continuity" is best manifested in Hailu's use of language and the method he has appropriated to structure his narrative. The language is poetic;

it is figurative, allegorical, and rich with proverbs. Hailu also makes effective use of (oral) poetry, which, imitating one of its several functions in Tigrinya oral tradition, he repeatedly adopts in the novel to punctuate a crisis or a transformation that the novel's hero is undergoing. At the sentence level, too, Hailu's language makes repeated use of the poetic devices of repetition and parallelism. All of these features are associated, primarily though not exclusively, with the art of oral tradition. Additionally, whereas the novel's story progresses linearly in time, Hailu's narrative proceeds by a traditional recursive technique of telling, which, subsequently, enables Hailu to structure the novel circularly. In fact, because the language of repetition and parallelism and the circular structure of the novel are so intertwined, the narrative structure of *The Conscript* echoes (or flows from) the poetic language of repetition and parallelism.

Hailu's engagement with oral tradition is also clear in the thematic content of the book. Whereas *The Conscript,* as a novel, is part of a modernist genre in the literary history of the Tigrinya language, the story it tells, the images and memory it evokes, and the songs it reproduces are deeply embedded in the oral tradition, and therefore in the collective consciousness, of the people of Eritrea. Such stories, even today, are passed on as part of the oral tradition from generation to generation in different versions and renderings. Even though the Libyan war described in the novel took place a century or so ago, many families in Eritrea tell stories of fathers or grandfathers or other relatives who were conscripted into the Italian military campaign in Libya. There are also similar stories of conscription that relate to colonial Italy's aggression toward Ethiopia from 1935 to 1941. Italy used Eritrean conscripts over an extended period of time to serve in different geographical spaces. There were thus two generations of conscripts. The first generation was sent to fight in Libya and Somalia from roughly 1910 to 1930; a second generation fought later in Ethiopia.[3] The number of Eritreans who served in the Libyan and Ethiopian campaigns was strikingly high, relative to the Eritrean population of about 600,000 in 1935.[4] Uoldelul Chelati writes that although, "in fact, often those [conscript] battalions were not composed exclusively of Eritreans but included soldiers from neighboring countries, particularly Ethiopia and Sudan," the estimations are that "approximately 130,000 Eritreans served in the Italian colonial army between the years 1890 and 1935 with an apex of roughly 60,000 during the campaign invasion of Ethiopia in 1935."[5] During my childhood and adult life in Eritrea, I heard many stories about both generations of conscripts, stories sometimes told by the veterans themselves. My father told stories about his experience as a conscript in Italy's campaign against Ethiopia (in 1935–41), where he ended up as a prisoner of war after the Italians surrendered to the British in Gondar, Ethiopia. Further back in time, my grandmother also told stories about her brother and his friends, who had undergone traumatic war experience in the earlier Libyan war.

Despite their essential historical and cultural importance, however, the oral versions of conscription that have circulated in the Eritrean culture tend to highlight certain features of the conscription history while glossing over other important aspects of the experience. *The Conscript* complicates those stories, evoking a historical and cultural memory that makes for a complex picture of the conscription experience at different levels. In *The Conscript,* Hailu provides a counterpoint to correct local Eritrean perceptions that either celebrate the conscripts as heroes or dismiss them as dupes. In creating Tuquabo, the central hero of the novel, who rebels against colonialism, he tells the untold story of those conscripts who resisted Italian colonialism but were forced to fight. Though Hailu creates a dissident central character to expose the evils of European colonialism on the African continent, his concurrent acknowledgement of an African native complicity—very clearly articulated in the novel—shows the tragic reality in which the colonized found themselves under colonialism. Ultimately, it is this deep understanding and analysis of the evils of colonialism—that is, the abuse and misuse of the colonized—that makes *The Conscript* distinct and important in the world of African literature. By the same token, it is the unapologetic ethical audacity to speak the truth to colonial power that defines Hailu's genius as one of the earliest literary voices of African literature.[6]

As a last remark, let me also say a few words about the translation process. The project has been on my mind for a long time. Although I had worked on the project in fits and starts in previous years, this translation was completed during an intense work period of eight weeks in the winter months of November–December 2010. Working on the first translation draft of *The Conscript* (and the many subsequent revisions) has been as exciting as it has been intricate. I have spent many hours blissfully thinking, translating, revising, and editing the text. Beyond the pleasure that is associated with finding the "right" words, expressions, and syntax, all of which are crucial to render meaning from one language to another, translation has also helped me better understand how Hailu's text is held together by linguistic subtleties, both verbal and structural, and by a parodying voice, a voice prevalent throughout the text and also one that Hailu articulates early on in the book when he speaks in the preface of an "ironic contrast." In this translation, my effort has been to truthfully render the form, meaning, and voice of the Tigrinya original in the English text. My hope is that this translation does justice to Hailu's extraordinary work, as it reaches now an English-reading audience, more than half a century since its first publication in Tigrinya.

Finally, I want to acknowledge the unconditional love and support of my family throughout the translation process. My heartfelt thanks also go to my friends and colleagues Steve Howard, Geri Lipschultz, Alemseged Tesfai, and Charles Cantalupo, and to my research assistant, Elizabeth Story, who read and gave me valuable feedback on the manuscript. I am deeply grateful to the members of the editorial staff at Ohio University Press for championing the manuscript and for their caring and enthusiastic production of the book. This book would never have become what it is without the editorial guidance of Gill Berchowitz, who gave me both time to work on it and deadlines to work against.

Of course, all mistakes and errors of judgment in this translation are mine.

This book is dedicated to my mother, Wahed, who always saw the wisdom in all, and my father, Negash, who saw the humor in everything.

Ghirmai Negash
June 2012

Notes

1. This section about Gebreyesus Hailu is taken almost verbatim from the biographical entries provided in "Gabra Yasus Haylu," *Encyclopedia Aethiopica* (2005), 630–31; and Abba Agostinos-Tedla, *La Lingua Abbisina* (Asmara: Edizioni "Adveniat Regnum Tuum," 1994), xii. See also Hailu's preface to the novel, in which he speaks about his journey to Italy.

2. Harold Scheub, "A Review of African Oral Traditions and Literature," *African Studies Review* 28, no. 2/3 (1985): 1.

3. For a fuller historical account of the different periods of conscription of Eritreans in the Italian colonial army, see Uoldelul Chelati Drar, "From Warriors to Urban Dwellers: *Ascari* and the Military Factor in the Urban Development of Colonial *Eritrea,*" *Cahiers d'études africaines* 175 (2004): 533–74; and Zemhret Yohannes, *Italiyawi Megza'ati ab Ertra: 1882–1941* (Asmara: Hdri, 2010), 373–76.

4. Drar, "From Warriors to Urban Dwellers," 549.

5. Ibid.

6. Parts of this section have appeared in my essay "Gebreyesus Hailu," in *Dictionary of African Biography,* ed. Emmanuel K. Akyeampong and Henry Louis Gates (Oxford: Oxford University Press, 2011).

Introduction

Laura Chrisman

Chinua Achebe's *Things Fall Apart* was, until recently, widely regarded as the first major African novel, with supporting roles given to other 1950s African works by Camera Laye, Mongo Beti, Amos Tutuola, and Ferdinand Oyono. The canonization of Achebe's 1958 Nigerian work, written in English and published by the London publisher Heinemann, had many serious consequences. One was the neat association of aesthetic with state processes. The publication of Achebe's novel during Nigeria's emerging independence from British rule reinforced a view that African literature only properly came into being with postcolonial sovereignty. Canonization of Achebe's novel also sanctioned European languages as the unquestioned medium of African literature. Over the last fifteen years, however, scholars have begun major revision of African literary history. The assumption that African fiction properly began in the postwar era of decolonization has given way to a far less tidy, but far more historically accurate, understanding that in Africa, as in other parts of the European imperial world, colonized writers were engaged in producing important and original fiction long before their countries succeeded in the struggle for self-determination. *Things Fall Apart* is increasingly treated now as inaugurating the institutionalization of African literature within the Euro-American metropole, rather than inaugurating the literary field itself.

Scholars, and publishers, are energetically pursuing the archival expansion that this new literary history mandates. For instance, they are discovering and reprinting African texts from the nineteenth century, such as Joseph Walter's *Guanya Pau* and the anonymous *Marita, or the Folly of Love.* Accompanying the growth of archive is the growth of conceptual and theoretical enquiry. In different ways, anti- and post-colonial thinkers from Frantz Fanon to Homi K. Bhabha earlier fueled critical assumptions that imperialism, as an ideological/discursive domain, exercised nearly total control over the cognitive horizons of colonized elites, writers, and intellectuals. This has given way to new analysis that accords both more agency to colonized subjects and more diversity to their cultural, political, and identity formations. Recognizing that these developed not only through the metropolitan-imperial axis but also through horizontal flows to other colonized and racially subordinated populations, scholars are re-evaluating the nature of transnationalism itself. At the same time, scholars are now reconsidering the spaces within the colony; in particular, they are giving fresh scrutiny to the ideological and material relationships between early African writing practices and European missions.

If African literary studies are rapidly expanding their historical and conceptual understanding, the pace of linguistic expansion in the field has been comparatively slow, despite Ngugi wa Thiong'o's ongoing and powerful argument, over the last thirty years, for authors and critics to prioritize writing in African vernacular languages. Anglophone and Francophone African literatures continue to dominate scholarly attention, at least within the metropole. However, there is growing institutional recognition of the Lusophone and Hispanophone literatures of Angola, Mozambique, and Equatorial Guinea (and, to some extent, the Afrikaans literature of South Africa). Outside of dedicated translators and specialists, however, African language literatures remain largely overlooked as the major cultural expressions that they are.

For these reasons this publication of *The Conscript,* Hailu's major Tigrinya novel, is most timely. Its translation into English helps to reverse the continuing Europhone bias of African literary studies and contributes to the continuing expansion of the historical literary archive. It was composed in 1927, a decade that saw major Europhone and indigenous African fiction (as well as poetry) enter into print. Black South African authors were especially active, producing such Anglophone novels as Sol Plaatje's 1930 novel *Mhudi* (written in 1920) and R. R. R. Dhlomo's 1929 novel *An African Tragedy,* as well as Thomas Mofolo's 1925 Sesotho novel *Chaka* and John Dube's 1930 Zulu novel *Jeqe, Shaka's Body Servant.* Of these four, only Dhlomo's has a contemporary setting; the other three are historical novels set in the early nineteenth century. In comparison, Hailu's work is startling for its openly anticolonial stance, modernist style, and international subject matter, Italy's use of Eritrean soldiers in its war of Libyan conquest.

Hailu paints a devastating portrait of European colonialism. As well as exposing the operations of foreign domination, he confronts the obstacles to liberation for which the colonized Eritreans themselves are responsible, highlighting both their material and subjective collusion with their own exploitation. At the same time that he develops this critique, Hailu celebrates the potential for resistant consciousness, which he sees as already present, albeit embryonically, in existing Eritrean social, cultural, and spiritual formations.

Hailu's approach to colonialism anticipates the midcentury thinkers Frantz Fanon and Aimé Césaire. Like them, Hailu is concerned less with imperial history than with its contemporary expression; the Italian empire is in medias res, like the protagonist Tuquabo himself at the start of the novel. The details of how Italy came to colonize Eritrea and to declare war on Libya are immaterial to the narrative; instead, Hailu simply remarks, "This was a time when there was war going on in Tripoli, and it was deemed fitting for the people of *Habesha* to be willing to spill their blood in this war" (7). The passive construction is interesting. Italian agency is missing here, and this absence becomes all the more glaring when the next sentence reads, "The youth were singing, 'He is a woman who refuses to go to Libya,' and small children in return sang, 'Come back to us later, Tribuli . . . give us time to grow up,' dispersing their poisonous words" (7). Hailu chooses to emphasize the prowar activities of local Eritrean youth, children, and also "those *Habesha* chiefs" who pray for war on the grounds that "the exercise might help trim their fattened bodies" (7). (Sixty years later, in Ken Saro-Wiwa's novel *Sozaboy,* the decision of the eponymous Sozaboy to enlist in the Nigerian Civil

War is likewise influenced by a cross-generational spread of local men who promote a particular brand of masculinity.)

Like Fanon and Césaire, Hailu highlights the dehumanization at the core of colonial domination. Césaire emphasizes the dehumanization of European perpetrators: "the colonizer, who in order to ease his conscience gets into the habit of seeing the other man as an animal, accustoms himself to treating him like an animal, and tends objectively to transform *himself* into an animal" (177). Hailu complicates this equation by featuring both colonizer and colonized as animals. In chapter 2, as the *ascari* prepare to board the train that will take them to war, the military police beat the crowds "with a whip (yes, with a whip like a donkey)." It is the train carriages, the apparatus of empire, that are explicitly bestialized: "the black trucks . . . roared like starving lions, hungry to swallow the *Habesha* people in their beastly bellies" (12). After the soldiers have entered combat and protected the Italians' access to water from other thirsty conscripts like themselves, they resemble servile "dogs," in the narrator's estimation, "whose eyes, while one is eating, are raised and lowered following the movement of one's hand" (46). From dogs they sink still further, in the view of the Italian general who abandons them in the Libyan desert, fearful that they will turn against and kill him: "For the Italian, the *Habesha* was like a weak donkey, which you couldn't kill for meat or hide and therefore would leave behind to die in the field under God's hand. The cowardly Italian, who gained his pride and fame from the strong young *Habesha,* thus escaped when he knew that they were weakened and dying of thirst" (47).

When the few survivors return to Eritrea by train, the same crowd that gathered to bid them farewell now gathers to welcome them, again enduring beating by the station's clerks and guards. By this time, the crowd itself is likened to animals: "When, after a while, the conscripts came out lined up on one side of the train, they were flooded by the crowd. The crowd seemed like growling sheep or goats which ran about to fetch their little ones, bucking and hitting anything on their way, while the little lambs moaned and jumped to find their mothers. There was noise, chaos, tears, and calling out of names on all sides as people fought to find their loved ones" (54). Colonialism creates a chaos of atomization among the colonized; Hailu uses animal epithets here in order to underscore the loss of human collectivity, which is also a loss of Eritrean national and local community. The self-destructive outcome of this dehumanization is demonstrated again and again, through the stampedes that feature in the first train station scene (12) and most violently in the desert (48), when desperate soldiers discover water.

However, neither atomization nor collusion wholly defines Eritrean people under Italian rule. Hailu represents resistance as emerging in sync with the war itself. If Eritreans have passively acquiesced in Italian colonization of their nation, the international export of their people as cannon fodder triggers an opposition that takes strength from long-standing social and cultural formations. Tuquabo's parents lament his decision to become a soldier, seeing in it a rejection of sacred family ties: "We feel orphaned. Why do you wish to fight for a foreigner? What use is it for you and your people to arm yourselves and fight overseas?" (8). His community augments this by cursing him for his betrayal of this familial-social contract: 'What a cruel son! How could he leave his old parents behind" (8). And there are martial precedents for insurgent consciousness: the *Habesha* are said to "have pride in their history and land, . . . [and] a long history of resistance" (28).

In themselves, the resources of historic martial valor, patriotic pride, and communitarianism may be necessary, but they are not sufficient to successfully counteract the Italian empire. These belong to an ethos and an era that is, Hailu suggests, inadequate to the violence of colonial modernity. Only the battlefield experience can dialectically bring forth an anticolonial awareness sufficient to translate, potentially, into a liberationist practice. Modern resistant consciousness begins to take form as a mysterious "anonymous, internal voice," which arises when the conscripts first set up camp in the Libyan desert and attempt to sleep, and warns them that "the Arabs are not your enemies. Will you be able to recognize your true enemy?" (21). It does not take much time after that for soldiers such as Tuquabo to arrive at a fuller understanding that builds on this intimation. This anonymous voice is an intriguingly original device through which Hailu synthesizes contemporary psychology and a more archaic mode of divine intercession.

The nativist sociocultural formations that Hailu invokes combine progressive and regressive impulses. Among the latter, Hailu points to xenophobia and antiblack color prejudice as directed against the Sudanese. Hailu draws selectively upon the progressive elements while rejecting the regressive, a practice theorized and recommended by anticolonial activist Amilcar Cabral, in such speeches as "National Liberation and Culture". He does this to clear the space for a multiethnic, multifaith African political community, founded upon global humanist understanding and shared opposition to European empire. This understanding develops dialectically through the course of the novel, as the soldiers travel across Eritrea by train, along the Red and Mediterranean Seas by ship, then by foot across the Libyan Desert. Hailu's vision is simultaneously national and international, then, and as such confirms Fanon's radical argument about their interdependency: "The building of his nation . . . will necessarily lead to the discovery and advancement of universalizing values. Far then from distancing it from other nations, it is the national liberation that puts the nation on the stage of history. It is at the heart of national consciousness that international consciousness establishes itself and thrives. And this dual emergence, in fact, is the unique focus of all culture" (180). Some thirty years later, writing from within an antinationalist academic environment, Edward Said's *Culture and Imperialism* echoes this analysis: "There is . . . a consistent intellectual trend within the nationalist consensus that is vitally critical, that refuses the short-term blandishments of separatist and triumphalist slogans in favour of the larger, more generous human realities of community *among* cultures, peoples, and societies. This community is the real human liberation portended by the resistance to imperialism" (217).

Hailu's representation of nationhood both overlaps with and departs from Benedict Anderson's influential 1983 analysis of nationalism, *Imagined Communities.* Of the conscripts, Hailu writes that "all of them, together, were thinking about their country at the same time" (16) as they travel on ship; when they awake the next day, the land is still visible, "which made them happy even though they didn't know the place. It was a vast piece of land that linked with and formed part of their country" (16).

This synchronized conjuring of, and attachment to, a shared space beyond knowable locality somewhat corresponds to Anderson's account of the nation as "imagined because the members of even the smallest nation will never know most of their fellow-members, meet them, or even hear of them, yet in the minds of each lives the image of their communion" (6). But rather than unknown humans, it is the unknown land itself that provides the foundation for their imagined communion and identity. When it comes to the human members of this space, Hailu offers particularity, not abstract generality: "Those with parents and siblings and those with wives and children were absorbed in their memories. Those who did not leave behind families thought of their friends or people who were close to them" (16). The shared physical landmass mediates heterogeneous human networks, in a dialectic that is absent from Anderson. Of those networks, it should be remarked that Hailu's novel consistently features a variety of primary affective relations. The protagonist Tuquabo's primary relationship is with his parents; for the bereaved woman who features towards the end of the book, her significant relative is her deceased brother. At no point does Hailu endow romantic or marital relationships with an elevated social or ethical significance, nor advocate a rigid gender hierarchy. Arguably, his approach delinks the projects of patriarchy and nationalism and criticizes the version of masculinity that prompts Tuquabo to fight. There is little support in the novel for viewing the nation through the ideological lens of heterosexual reproduction, a view that feminists have critiqued for reducing women to the role of biological reproducers, cultural transmitters, or symbolic abstractions of the nation.

If the land mediates national identity, for Hailu, the sea (helped by God) mediates international identity. The novel's narrative logic is too complex for detailed discussion here. It involves the spiritual framing of the sea as a sublime, humbling power that causes the soldiers to appreciate the "expansiveness of the human race and culture inhabiting the world" (19) and to become critical of the ethnocentric insularity that frequently accompanies landlocked existence. Hailu celebrates and calls for cosmopolitan connection and exchange in a way that does not seek to erase but rather to complement national, cultural, and religious differences. He positions international Christianity (in the form of the Coptic Church) as a historical precedent for a future pan-Africanism, less for doctrinaire than for pragmatic reasons. For the Eritrean soldiers who sail on this ship, their biblical knowledge works to identify, authorize, and venerate the foreign geography and ancient monuments that they encounter as they travel north. Their encounter with the Suez Canal provides the positive emblem of a modernity that enables Asian and African connection, accomplished through "the ingenious Frenchman Ferdinand de Lesseps" (20). As such, the canal, and de Lesseps, contrast in chapter 2 with the city of Asmara, which the Italians are said to have made "perfect," "beautiful and affecting," "with well-made streets and roads lined with trees on each side" (11). This opening affirmative portrait of Asmara immediately gives way to Hailu's horrific train station scene, where, as previously discussed, train carriages devour soldiers and the station unleashes violent chaos. What the Suez scene reveals is that the modern technology introduced by Europe is not problematic in itself; the problem lies with the imperial social relations which it has accompanied.

Egypt had already obtained political independence in 1922, which makes the Suez Canal available for Hailu's recuperation as a progressive icon of pan-African potential. If the French, through de Lesseps, can now be lauded for their (unintended) contribution to this political possibility, Hailu can only condemn the Italians for their ongoing efforts to divide and rule. They effect this not only through physical force but also through social engineering and propaganda. One of the most unusual sections of the novel is its discussion of Arab stereotypes (32–35). It seems odd that Hailu should devote so many pages to replicating these ugly stereotypes without judgment. But a closer reading reveals this to be a clever and subtle form of anticolonial argument. As the narrator points out, it is the Italians who are responsible for spreading these accounts of Arab "laziness," which are refuted by their activity as soldiers in defending Libya against colonization. The Arab bravery that Tuquabo observes firsthand exposes the fictitiousness of colonial representation and confirms what Fanon might call the "social truth" of praxis.

The operation of textuality is of broad interest to Hailu, whose own writing is constantly dynamic, shifting around between first, second, and third person without transition (though always with purpose), incorporating proverbs, song, contemporary cinematic snapshot techniques, and nineteenth-century Italian poetry. The mixing of genre and voice accompanies an equally dynamic approach to time and place; the novel opens in medias res, as previously observed, with Tuquabo departing for war, flashes back to his birth and childhood, returns to the present, distills two years of conscription, and ends in an indeterminate temporal zone, past the death of his mother:

"Some days later, Tuquabo asked to be discharged from the Italian army and returned to his village. His father didn't live much longer, and the death of his mother continued to be the most painful experience for him for a long time to come" (57). Movement through space has particular thematic prominence throughout the book (and begins in the author's preface, which locates the novel's origins in his sea voyage to Italy). Tuquabo is constantly on the move. Long before he becomes a soldier, travels by train, travels by ship, travels by foot in the desert, we watch him as a child accompany his father on periodic overnight trips to their cattle, while the nearby birds and baboons are also on the move (6). We also witness the movement of the crowds in the station, the illusory movement of Eritrean mountains away from the ship (15), the movement of dolphins swimming around the ship (17), the movement of Libyan nomads (30), the movement of soldiers in battle. Hailu connects movement of and through physical matter to the movement of emotions and of sound, all of which combine and culminate in the excessively beating heart of Tuquabo's mother, which causes an artery to rupture while she calls her son's name (51). Like Fanon, Hailu gets at his political analysis through a phenomenological examination of memory, emotions, imagination, and the senses, in which, for Hailu, the human heart plays a central, unifying role, as does human song. In his approach to affect, as with his exploration of the impact of natural environment on human consciousness, Hailu anticipates twenty-first-century critical trends in the humanities.

For all its thematic and stylistic commitment to the dynamic flux of consciousness, *The Conscript* is also a carefully composed and formally disciplined work. Hailu favors the structural devices of parallelism (it is again the author's preface that initiates this pattern, pairing *The Conscript* with his long poem *Emperor Tewedros's Suicide*). The chaotic Asmara train station scene occurs near the beginning and end of the novel; so does Tuquabo's benediction/malediction. Hailu twins a traditional Eritrean song (15) with the poem by Leopardi (23); both express similar sentiments in support of "home" and against exile. Pointedly, and ironically, it is the Italian poem that is more openly antiwar; Hailu uses Italian aesthetic culture against itself, to critique Italian imperial militarism. The point of these parallelisms lies as much in their contrasts as in their repetitions. By the concluding train scene, Eritrean clerks have internalized the colonizer's propensity for violence, as has the crowd; by the time the novel ends, Tuquabo wishes to be cursed, not blessed. His final dirge is an extended synthesis of the Tigrinya and Leopardi poems. Unlike those, however, this song makes possible an alternative future by breaking with the past: "I am done with Italy and its tribulations / . . . / Farewell to arms!" (57).

Works Cited

Anderson, Benedict. *Imagined Communities: Reflections on the Origin and Spread of Nationalism.* New edition. New York: Verso, 2006.

Cabral, Amilcar. "National Liberation and Culture." In *Colonial Discourse and Post-Colonial Theory: A Reader,* edited by Patrick Williams and Laura Chrisman, 53–65. New York: Columbia University Press, 1994.

Césaire, Aimé. "From *Discourse on Colonialism.*" In *Colonial Discourse and Post-Colonial Theory: A Reader,* edited by Patrick Williams and Laura Chrisman, 172–80. New York: Columbia University Press, 1994.

Fanon, Frantz. *The Wretched of the Earth.* Translated by Richard Philcox. New York: Grove Press, 2004.

Said, Edward. *Culture and Imperialism.* New York: Vintage, 1996.

Preface to the Tigrinya Edition

This book which is being printed under the title *A Story of a Conscript* reflects my impressions when, at the age of eighteen, I traveled by sea to Italy to seek an education. It is also about the memory of my fellow-countrymen, the *ascari* recruits, who were traveling overseas at that time. And that is why my writing is of a young person, and also the reason why I have kept the original name that was given to me at the time of my birth. I consider myself a blessed person and thank my God for enabling me to express the concerns and feelings of my people at that young age.

This work could not be published until now for want of means. Today, however, the book is being published with the loan I received from the Ethiopian-Eritrean Unity Association. I express my gratitude to them.

There is also another piece entitled *Emperor Tewodros's Suicide,* which I wrote in the same period I worked on *A Story of a Conscript.* It is a tragedy in sixteen hundred lines of verse. That work awaits the day when it will see publication. Those who are judicious enough to compare will see that there is a vivid, ironic contrast between them: on one end of the scale, the one who sacrifices himself for his country, and, on the other end of the scale, the one who dies fighting another man's war, in foreign lands.

Dr. A. G. Hailu

The Conscript

ONE

A Portrait of Youth

He put down his gun beside him, knelt down before his parents, and asked: "My mother and father bless me, for I do not know what my fate will be in Tripoli." Tuquabo was dressed in a gray uniform with a colorful belt that embellished his waist, and from his ankle to his knee was bandaged with a thick strip of cloth that looked like a horse blanket. Overwhelmed with emotion, his parents were speechless. They looked at their son's uniform, which they had never seen before, with eyes filled with admiration and shock. They were both older by now. Tuquabo's father was in his mid-seventies, his mother in her late sixties. But if anyone were to guess their ages at that moment, they would each gain ten years. Their faces were worry-stricken, their eyes were hollow, and their brows skinny.

Tuquabo was their only son. This does not mean they had not borne other children; all the other five children had been taken by God long ago. This seeming rivalry with death caused great anxiety in them. When he was small, God almost took Tuquabo too.

Just a few weeks after his birth, his mother took him to the village church. Forbidden to enter the church out of custom, because she was still recovering from labor, she stood in the compound cradling her newborn; eyes full of tears, she prayed and begged. "Jesus, my Lord, the savior of the world, you have already taken many children from me; as you can see, I am an old woman and can no longer bear children. Jesus, be kind, show mercy. Please leave this one child for us so that when his father and I get old he can be our cane and eyes. I beg you to give this one as a gift." Already weakened by her labor and trembling with emotion and maternal feeling, her head began spinning and she felt dizzy. She soon recovered and went back home with a strong feeling of hope for her child. On arriving home, she dozed off into a deep sleep that was filled with dreams. Her son was lying on her breast all the time. In her dream, she saw herself in a wonderful wilderness. She saw six flowers, called *hawohawo* (haemantus), waving with the wind. As she came closer to the flowers, admiring their beauty, she saw an unknown hand with a sickle plucking them away one by one. Shocked by the incident, she stood frozen as the sickle continued cutting off the remaining flowers. When the sickle approached the sixth flower, an unseen person moved it away so that it would not be cut off. The action was repeated three times. Then, as she wondered anxiously about what was happening, she suddenly saw a handsome figure clad with bright light. "The vision you saw is a symbol of your children. Five have died. I am sparing you the last one. I am Medhaniye Alem, the One who you trust and prayed to," he said, and disappeared. She woke up with disbelief and joy; the boy woke up crying, and, after a long period of illness, he started breastfeeding eagerly as he had never done before. She hardly believed her luck as she kept kissing him. Hot tears of joy came down her cheeks, and she thanked her God for his kindness and mercy for keeping her son alive. Over time her son grew strong and healthy. And on the day of his baptism, his mother insisted that he be named Tuquabo Medhaniye Alem (God's gift) for receiving a great blessing from her God. And so they named him. His father was called Habte-Mikael, and his mother, Tek'a.

Tuquabo Medhaniye Alem, or Tuquabo as he was called, because people like to shorten names, grew up into a robust young man cultivating his talents at home and in the fields. He loved and respected people. He expressed his love for his mother often by hugging her around the neck, embracing her, and pouring sweet and loving words upon her. He delighted his father by being with him, doing chores, and learning the names of his ancestors from him. At dusk, his father would play with him by testing if he knew his pedigree, and ask him, "Who is your father," to which Tuquabo would answer, "I am Habte-Mikael's son," to the father's expectant joy. His father would add more to the list, each time teaching him more. "Habte-Mikael is the son of Hidru; Hidru was the son of Red'ai . . ." It was pleasing to see Tuquabo, the child, playing with his parents this way and growing to become the source of happiness in the house. As he grew older, his father sent him to school. He was a quick learner and excelled beyond his peers in memorizing what his teachers taught him, and in not forgetting what he had learned. But he was also growing as a *Habesha*, and he developed an interest in weaponry and the military. Regarding this, his father was delighted and encouraged him to be brave, promising that this sword or that spear would be his later. There is a Tigrinya proverb that says that "a razor is created with a sharp edge," and it reminded Tuquabo's father of his son's valor and intelligence in handling the weaponry, which made him proud. Tuquabo's mother also took pride in her son's bravery and ability; whose mother wouldn't? But she was also worried about it. Her mind was haunted by concerns that her son would die in war one day, and where would he go to fight? Would he ever come back once he left for war? Unable to quiet her mind, she would try to appeal to her husband, but to no avail. He would constantly dismiss her saying, "Don't be silly . . . it should give us joy to see the bravery of our son . . . not sadness." His mother would calm her fears by completely relying upon her God to protect her son from every calamity or disaster.

They were a rich family with abundant cattle, and they hired a Moslem family to look after them. Sometimes Tuquabo and his father would go to the Saho Moslem family overnight to look after the well-being of their cattle. When they traveled, Tuquabo, more than anything else, loved the mule ride, when his father sang and told stories, and the rhythmic motion of the mule, smoothly floating on the plains, carried them along, like water running on the ground. As a child, Tuquabo was riveted by the sudden movement of flying birds, and shuffling sounds in the bush would make his heart throb. As they rode by, they might see a flock of baboons, and Tuquabo would laugh at the sight of a monkey's swift jump away from them. In his young heart, he wondered about why the baboons, so strong in numbers, were running away from them, but he kept such thoughts to himself. After reaching their destination, to be entertained with milk and porridge by their Saho Moslem friends, they would enjoy themselves under a full moon and listen to the chewing of the cattle. The silence was now and then broken by the ugly baying of the hyenas and the barking and yelping of dogs, which amazed and frightened Tuquabo. All these impressions he easily absorbed and preserved in his clear and innocent heart for a time later in life when he would leave for another country so that his homeland might remain a treasure in his memory. On returning home from such trips with his father, Tuquabo would cling to his mother and tell those stories to her.

This was a time when there was war going on in Tripoli, and it was deemed fitting for the people of *Habesha* to be willing to spill their blood in this war. The youth were singing, "He is a woman who refuses to go to Libya," and small children in return sang, "Come back to us later, Tribuli . . . give us time to grow up," dispersing their poisonous words. Tuquabo was listening to all of these. Since he was a very bright boy, he would question all these issues in his mind. After a while, for someone born at this period of time, it happened gradually that all the songs and information were stamped on his heart. As it is a fact that what you hear during your childhood becomes clearer as you get older, he resolved to go to Libya to fight as a hero and gain fame. He resolved so just because he heard that there was war going on there. His ambition may also have been influenced by those *Habesha* chiefs who said they hated to sit idle after a brief break from going to war. They begged, "Lord, don't let us be dormant, please bring us war." Their eagerness was evident in their boastful saying that the exercise might help trim their fattened bodies. In any event, once decided, Tuquabo began to talk less and isolate himself more. His mother sensed something in the air and began to incessantly question him, but his only reply was "What are you saying, Mother . . . nothing is going on . . ." He avoided his mother's scrutiny and shifted his eyes around, fearing exposure of what was in his heart.

One night he left home and joined the army as a conscript bound for Tripoli. To feel and imagine the distress he created for his parents, let anyone who is a parent or who has parents fathom the intensity. In the beginning they couldn't believe or accept the reality of the event, but later they let out all their tears and remained in deep sadness. It was to no avail. He was now in the hands of the heartless Italians, and there was no way they could get him back.

When the day came for departure, his parents decided to see their son for the last time, and walked slowly to the train station. They stood beside their son, and, as we saw him at the beginning, he knelt down and waited for their blessings. They were silent for some time but then forced out words. "You were our light and joy. We feel orphaned. Why do you wish to fight for a foreigner? What use is it for you and your people to arm yourselves and fight overseas? You have all you want, why? But what can we say; it's all God's wish. Go, and may our Lord protect you and give you strength. As for us, we are old people, beaten by sorrow, and we may not survive your return after two years. We hope to see you again, but all is in God's hands." After they had blessed him, but before they could kiss him goodbye very well, the guards snatched him from their embrace. His mother, catching sight of her son sobbing terribly, could not contain herself and fainted. She would have fallen to the ground if not for the support of her husband. The people around were all touched by this and couldn't control their tears. "What a cruel son! How could he leave his old parents behind?" They were cursing him. Tuquabo kept looking at his mother and heard the curses of the crowd; the world turned upside down for him, and he ran away from them. He wanted to bury himself under the ground. His father was meekly pleading with the crowd not to curse their son, but to bless him instead. His mother, because she had fainted, missed the curses upon her son. It would have been painful for her to hear. Had she been able to speak, she would have concurred with the father's pleas. They loved their son so much. They went back to their village and were overtaken by suffering, driven by sorrow. Darkness fell upon the house. It was like returning home after the funeral of a beloved one.

TWO

The Departure from Asmara

Asmara is a city built in the Hamasien region on a plain. Someone who sees it from Ras Alula Palace finds it beautiful and affecting. The coming of the Italians made it perfect, with well-made streets and roads lined with trees on each side. One day around noon, on the road that leads to the train station, there were many people hurriedly making their way. One person inquired of another why thousands of people were passing by. "It is today that the soldiers are going to Tribuli. Let's go and see." Another was saying that it is not really appealing to see people wailing in their misery and sadness. Anyone who doesn't feel a pinch in that situation really is devoid of human feeling. Many people were crowded around the train. In the middle of the crowd, people were calling for their beloveds, and those unable to find their loved ones were in a state of despair. It was such a pitiful moment, and on more than one occasion people would spot someone from a distance and barge through the crowd treading on people's feet just to see their loved one, provoking a load of insults and curses from hurting and tearful folks. Some people had prepared food and drinks for their loved ones and were looking out for them. Upon seeing the tumultuous crowd, they felt hopeless and just stood there. Some others would spot each other and run to be together, and the military police would intervene and beat them with a whip (yes, with a whip like a donkey). If they saw each other from a distance, they would say farewell and give their blessings to each other using hand gestures. But the most disturbing aspect of the scene was the black trucks that roared like starving lions, hungry to swallow the *Habesha* people in their beastly bellies. They were blaring, honking, and wailing, while women sang together a melancholy song, "The train comes smoking and your mother's daughter is crying." With the train station still filled with a frenzy of a sobbing and wailing public, the confusion and disturbance were beyond imagining.

Later on, the Italian military officers came to notify the soldiers of their readiness to depart. The noise of the crowd intensified, and the military police started beating people again. The wailing and screaming grew even louder. It was heard everywhere. There began a stampede, and many women fell, with no one there to help them up. Not five minutes later, the blowing of the trumpet sounded, and nobody spoke for a few minutes. When the soldiers started to board the trains, people began to feel tense again. The metal doors closed, and trains started their engines in a smug, slow motion, showing their pride in what they were doing, as if to say they knew they were indeed taking the best sons of the land. The conscripts were waving their scarves, saying, "Good-bye, my land, I'm going to Tripoli." They were singing as they disappeared into the horizon. This was a final farewell, for many of them would not make it back.

The black train zigzagged down the winding slopes and mountains. As it carried the conscripts deep down the twisting gorges, the train seemed like an evil force driving some miserable creatures to hell. Among them was Tuquabo Habte-Mikael. From Arbe-Rebu'e till Nefasit and Embatkala, they observed the greenery, lush hills, and winding paths. But after a while they reached far beyond Ghinda, where they were greeted by a dry land. Having raced through the semidesert plains for the whole afternoon, the train finally dropped them off them in Massawa when darkness was falling. The sea, looking full of smoke because of the mist and fog, lay before them.

For the conscripts it was their first time at the seaside. Tuquabo and the rest were overwhelmed by the sight. It is true that the sea is a mystery for a person looking at it for the first time. The sensation that you have at that time cannot be passed on, nor can it be adequately expressed in words. It has the appearance of an infinitely vast field, gray at dusk and dawn, alternating with a greenish color during the day. In fact, you don't know what your heart feels when you stand before the view: it feels like you are a dreamer looking at some magnificence, and you are dumbfounded by it. Many thoughts run into your mind, and desires as well. A desire that cannot be contained; you feel like running and jumping into the sea? Oh no . . . how about fear? Where should it go? Unable to control yourself, you cry (what can I say) and laugh at the same time. To praise the God who created this perfect beauty, your heart flies up to the skies on high. You feel un-expressed euphoria, which I think you might want to experience for eternity, craving a small amount every time. If the splashing of the water against the shore did not bring you to reality, it would seem like a dream world. The pleasure is so great. Waking up at dawn, you see the low tide waves of the sea splashing against each other as they meander like carefree goats, while the pleasant wind that blew from the sea strikes your face, cooling it off from the oven heat of Massawa. You also spot some fishing boats leaving to catch fish, with their nets cast (masts hoisted, too), at the same time that some of the big fish that come to the shallow waters closer to land to find food somersault away before the sun hits harder. This indeed is very pleasant to see. But furthermore, it also makes you feel as if you are witnessing what you read in the Gospel about the Sea of Tiberias, or the Lake of Gennesaret. It reminds you of Peter, Andreas, the sons of Zebedee, and Jesus Christ. All the conscripts felt that way.

The next day at nine in the evening it was time for boarding. The ship was ready to depart and gave out a thick smoke. The Italian officers seated themselves on an upper deck apart from the rest. As for the *Habesha,* they were stationed in the open, where there is no shelter from the sun's heat and rain, a place where you put animals.

The ship made thunderous noises as the engine moved. The sailors were busily running back and forth, some folding the stairs, others pulling up the heavy anchor from deep down the sea. At last, the guards patrolled the ship lest there was any person hiding. Everything was ready. The ship howled, emitting a sound that created cold shivers in your stomach, and moved slowly. The children of Ethiopia started singing. While one played the *kirar,* a left-handed boy was pounding a drum, making a deafening noise. Tuquabo was deep in thought, far away from the world of singing and dancing. From the deck of the ship he looked back towards his land. Thoughts of his mother and father dominated his mind, and Tuquabo saw Massawa running away from him. It is true that at nighttime on a ship it doesn't look like the ship is sailing, it feels like the land is moving away. Tuquabo felt emotionally stirred up when he saw his native land moving away. And feeling a lump in the throat, he said, "O my country that raised me in its green land and beautiful hills, I say farewell to you. The entire field that I once lived in with my cattle and shepherds . . . I say farewell to you."

> Go ahead,
> Leave your family and country behind
> For someone else's expanse
> That you don't want.
> Feel like a stranger
> Until you're dead.

Thinking of this traditional song, he regretted the day he was born. "It was my choice that I came here, so let me suffer the consequences," he said to himself with anger. Massawa was still moving away from him. The lights were dimming. The Ethiopian mountains looked like huge walls covered with mist. The water behind the ship was foaming and splashing, and seemed like a streaming river that was following them. On their left and right sides, they could see the last flickering red and green lights, which they took as a final reminder and salutation from their homeland. They kept on looking until the lights disappeared, giving way to pitch dark. Then all of them sank into deep thought. They felt forlorn. Those who were singing stopped without really being aware. They knew they were leaving their country. Even those strong young men who sometime before had appeared not to be vulnerable to anything that distracted their happiness were quiet now. They too sat down and struggled to sleep wherever they could lay their heads (no *n'edi* or mud bed for them now), merely covering themselves with their coats.

Especially those with parents and siblings and those with wives and children were absorbed in their memories. Those who did not leave behind families thought of their friends or people who were close to them. All of them, together, were thinking about their country at the same time. It is easier to imagine than to describe how fast their hearts were beating at that time. The memory of one's homeland can be overwhelming. Still, they eventually fell into some sort of sleep that night, a sleep that was interrupted by fits and starts of memories and dreams about their loved ones. When they woke up the next morning, they looked around them left and right. To their left, they saw the land of *habab,* which made them happy even though they didn't know the place. It was a vast piece of land that linked with and formed part of their country. Later on in the evening, they reached an expanse of sea from which no land could be seen. On all sides they were surrounded by water and the sky above them. Nothing else could be seen. They felt the heat. But there is a human tendency to divert one's attention from thinking about thirst when surrounded by water, and so, their minds eased by the view of the seawater, they did not seem particularly discomforted.

On the third day they arrived in Port Sudan, where the British were in power. Finally the droning ship lowered its anchor and stopped. Many dark and huge Sudanese people started to storm the ship. There, the two peoples, the Ethiopians and the Sudanese, came face to face. The latter were thinking, "These slaves! They are going to Tribuli for money!" while the former were thinking, "These black people! They could never be superior to us," both harshly judging each other. The ship left the port. The conscripts were expecting to see sea lions, fish that eat humans as they had heard about, but instead they saw dolphins swimming in the sea and around the ship. It is said that dolphins love humans. The reason that they swim after a ship is to save humans who might fall into the sea. It is said that Simonis was saved by dolphins, that they carried him back to his country, when he was thrown into the sea by his enemies. And some people say dolphins like to swim around a ship in case somebody throws food at them. Which one is the truth, I don't know. For the soldiers, all these things were new, and they were just observing in silence. The dolphins seemed to be singing songs of welcome and farewell, and appeared as though to mean, "We saw you off and walked you over across the river, and now we return home for our reward," a song girls in our land would sing when sending away a bridegroom to the bride's village. Whether they needed to save somebody or were searching for food, one couldn't know; but after that the dolphins returned to Port Sudan, jumping in and out of the water. The sun was setting by now, and a cool breeze came over and made the people feel alive.

It was pitch black in the middle of the sea. Ships that were passing by would therefore signal with lights as did the ship they were on. In all, the entire vision was astonishing. The most amazing part for them was the sight of the moon in the middle of the sea. When the sky and the sea were calm, in the direction of the East, from the side of the Arab countries, a dimly seen shrub-like and rounded object, but only viewed in half as in half of an *enjera,* sprouted from the water, at which all exclaimed in fear. They prayed, "In the name of God, the Son, and the Holy Spirit," and covered their faces. For them it seemed a scary phantasm and not a reflection of the moon that was coming out. All their attention was on the moon as it rose slowly, its light turning the water into red, making it look as if it were painted in blood. If some of them had been versed in the Bible and known the meaning of Eritrea is "red," they would have understood they were now in the Red Sea. Overwhelmed and spiritually uplifted, they would have recalled Moses's praise for the greatness of God. Finally, the moon came out fully and illuminated the whole sea, creating beautiful colors. In turn, like a petted cat that pleases by rubbing up its skin against a caring owner, the sea returned the moon's kindness by revealing its soothing waves. The moon grew brighter, further lighting up the sea. As the light fell on the conscripts and the ship sailed on, the moon also seemed to move at the same pace, as if tied to the ship by an invisible cord. I mean to say, it seemed to the conscripts that the moon also moved. The conscripts, especially those who came from the landlocked parts of Ethiopia, were in awe. They thought they were dreaming. Looking at the vastness of the sea, a moment where darkness turns to light, can only be clear to the mind which appreciates and experiences beauty and spirituality. Of the things that God created, the most beautiful one is the sea, which shows his immeasurable greatness. For this reason, those who are wise reflect and say, "My country is low and underdeveloped as compared with the rest of the world's kingdoms because it lacks the sea, which at the same time makes people closed off and ignorant."

After sailing the entire night, and the next day and evening as well, they reached a location near Egypt. They started arguing about where the Israelites crossed the sea; some of them said that this was the place, and others said it was not. Even though they were not sure of the spot, they knew the direction. Such discussion purely delights the Ethiopian heart, a heart which rejoices at the sight of God's greatness and respects and recalls the verses of the Holy Books. Amongst them, the learned ones were praising God by reciting verses in Ge'ez. From afar, the Arab hills could be seen with Mount Sinai in the midst, and they said, "O holy one, selected to be a staircase from heaven for God from all other hills, I humbly greet you," and they bowed towards the spot. An Ethiopian has respect for places named in the Bible. Anyway, the ship kept on sailing. Aware that they were moving farther and farther away from their land, they felt a storm of mixed feelings come over them. Now they had been at sea for the fourth day going on the fifth. The sea was getting shallower, and they saw the borderlands of Asia and Africa. Their heartbeats increased, and they greeted the land: "O you, the land, which is our neighbor and drinks from our river, the Nile, peace be to you."

The next day they arrived in the Arab town of Suez and were met by a crowd of Egyptians, some clad in colorful *jellabiyas* and others wearing khakis. They were selling dates, nuts, and sweets. The *Habesha* were fascinated by their encounter with the Egyptians and the activities around them, because knowing only their own people and dress custom, they had never before imagined the expansiveness of the human race and culture inhabiting the world. They left the town for the Suez Canal, which was a river-like narrow sea, and the ship sailed at a slow pace to the Egyptian town of Port Said. The Mediterranean Sea lay before them, with its swelling waves, and there stood at the entrance of the port a colossal figure of a man, standing lonely and firmly as though guarding the doorway. Afterward they learned that it was the monument to the ingenious Frenchman Ferdinand de Lesseps, who thought up the idea of connecting the Mediterranean Sea and the Red Sea by building a waterway. Their wonderment and awe were heightened by many new things they encountered, including the high buildings and the brightly lit streets, which were bustling with people, cars, and horse carts. When they entered the Mediterranean Sea, they were still able to catch sight of the African landscape on their left side, and, in fact, they caught sight of the city of Alexandria but didn't stop. They would have rejoiced to visit and pay tribute to Alexandria, and when they saw it from afar, they were thinking to themselves, "This is the holy city and home of the Patriarch of the Coptic Church, Patriarch Markos Eskenderia." The most thrilling thing was to notice how the *Habesha* were enthralled again when they saw the seat of the patriarch (as usual focusing on the good), but were ignorant of the wickedness of some of the patriarchs who were sent from that same place to Ethiopia and gave the people so much trouble.

Thereafter they headed briefly out to sea, before sailing along the African coast to reach the legendary town called Derna. This was to be their final destination. Now they knew the moment had arrived when their masculinity would be tested and many of them would meet their deaths. They descended from the ship, weighed down by agony and fear. They started trudging on the roasting sands of the Libyan Desert, and after awhile they stopped, set up their tents, and lay down to rest. They were already tired from the sea voyage, and they fell asleep quickly. And suddenly an anonymous, internal voice rose up, pricking the minds of the conscripts. “O my dear countrymen, who have come not to rest, have a rest. You need rest, for there is great work and hardship awaiting you in this hot country. The Arabs are watching from the horizon and telling each other, ‘Did you see the *Habesha* dog who sold his life for money! Let him be.’ Beware, *Habesha;* the Arabs are not your enemies. Will you be able to recognize your true enemy? What will they say to you? For now just try to rest.”

THREE

Deep in the Wilderness

> He who fights on a foreign soil another man's war
> Not for his family or his country's honor
> And, when he lies dying, hit by a deadly blow
> From an angry firearm
> But cannot say, "Oh! My beloved country
> Here is the life you gave me, I come back to you"
> Dies twice, reduced to eternal wretchedness.

This poem was written by Leopardi, a famous Italian poet. It could have been written for the *Habesha* conscripts. Having crossed the seas, the conscripts had now landed in the hot, dry wilderness, leaving behind their land, family, relatives, and friends. "Dear friend, do you think people live in this dry sand?" Tuquabo was asking, bewildered. "What can I say? I am just like you looking wherever my eyes take me to." "How can I know?" replied the other. Both fell silent. They were all silent; except for whispers and unfinished sentences, not even one song or meaningful word was heard in the entire group. The sense of shock, sadness, hopelessness, and regret was clearly visible on their faces. The view of the desert was overwhelming. There was not a single tree or blade of grass, not to speak of water. One could not possibly move in any direction—left, right, front, or back—for one found oneself always surrounded by sand, stone, gravel, and heaps of dust. It was an expanse like the sea, but a more hostile one. In the sea, you can see fish and listen to the sound of the waves. Not even a single chirping bird was heard, nor was a bird in flight seen in the desert. With the open cloudless sky, it was like a hot oven. The nausea created by the permanent blaze and the absence of breeze makes one wonder whether one is in the land of life or death. What a stark difference, when you think of the green, windy, fertile land of Ethiopia, where streams flow. All the conscripts were now saying, "I deserve this, for wanting to come here!" But there was nothing they could do about it except feel pity for themselves.

They had woken up in a sweat from their brief sleep. And as soon as the whistle for departure was blown, they somehow wiped their sweat and started walking slowly towards a place deep in the wilderness. But their feet were aching from sand burn, and some tried to tend their feet as much as they could, while others headed inland—hopping as a way to withstand the heat underneath. Those who owned shoes wore them, those who didn't improvised by wrapping pieces of cloth and handkerchiefs around their feet. That was useless. A make-do shoe was no match for the burning heat. The sand was like a glowing fire, with craters of hot ash everywhere. I recall one day myself running unawares into one of those hot ash craters. My legs sank up to my knees; I was full of burn wounds. Anyone who went through this experience like me will know; those who have not experienced it can, however, contemplate it with an open heart. It was through this hellhole that our countrymen were going, not for one day, but to live there for two years. Neither the shoes, nor the cloth with which they improvised to make shoes, could save them from the heat, as the sand that got into their shoes rendered the foot it covered bare. What can be said? Oh my God, it was devastating to see the wrath unleashed on them.

There is a Tigrinya adage which says, "The hyena that laughs at dawn is bound to cause havoc at dusk." For surely the beginning was agonizing, and the conscripts started asking each other what it was going to be like for two years if they were suffering this much already. Two years! Two years in such heat, in a land of hell, with a terrible wind blowing! Fine sand was ceaselessly blowing into their eyes, ears, and noses, making their lives miserable by slipping down into their bodies through their sleeves and necks. Their bodies were sweltering. Since it was very fine, the sand was even falling through onto their bellies. All that can be said is that it is probably from that same fine sand that the haze emerges that sometimes comes to our land, and it burns bodies, destroys our pastures, and emaciates our livestock. Do you see? How a sandstorm so hot—that even after it has traveled a long distance and been slowed down by vegetation and mild weather is able to cause drought and sickness when it reaches our homeland—would affect one who is in the midst of the place where it takes off from the blazing ground, where there is not a single tree for shade? In any case, who knows how many of them were falling ill?

The conscripts traveled for the whole day and rested in the evening. Their feet were burning with blisters and wounds. They slept on the sand without any carpet or cover, wearing their clothes, their ammunition bound to their bodies. For the Italian commanders who rode on mules for the whole day, a tent was put up to protect them from night cold and sandstorms. Their beds were prepared, and water was readied for them. And who was taking care of this? The wretched *Habesha,* whose lot is suffering. Is it not clear that it was the conscripts who most needed help and assistance? No, it was the *Habesha* who were destined to stand by the Italians when they were served supper, after slaving for them the whole day. It was also the *Habesha,* who were despicable to the Italian mind. And who else other than the *Habesha* was going to prepare their horses and pack their goods the next day in the morning? Well, there were more surprising things. When a son of *Habesha* was elected as a privileged orderly to serve a white man, whether it was making his bed, or preparing his sword and weapons, or cooking his food, or lighting his cigarette, he thought that he had reached seven skies higher than his colleagues. So the useless one who follows a mule and feels full by smelling its dung thinks he reigns as a king over his friends just because he has put a hat on his head. And so it went. As they spent the night scorched by the day's heat, stuffed with sand brought by winds, and were mocked by the night dew, they woke up the next day and moved on. Anyone who saw the conscripts then could see that their faces looked tattered, their eyes were red, and their lips were chapped. These young Ethiopians, whose faces had shone before as if they had been rubbed with butter, turned into such emaciated bodies in one day. It was hard to recognize them as Ethiopians at that time, but as useless persons from a cursed land. On the other hand, people back home were thinking about them, and cried, "Our priests, why don't you speak out? Not even one young man can be found; all have gone to Tripoli."

And at this time an internal voice spoke to Tuquabo. "Oh, poor Tuquabo! There was plenty of milk to drink, plenty of butter to eat in your home, but your parents have no one left to give their wealth to. You are dying of hunger and wasting away. Back home, when you returned from your trips your family welcomed you with a smile and showered you with blessings and everlasting joy. In your house, you were used to having hot water to wash feet, beer or aniseed drink to quench your thirst, a soft bed to sleep on, and you would sleep with your heart filled with joy. But now, where will you go to after spending all the day toiling? They do say, 'Don't go to a bad wife after spending the day with a bad ox.' This has now happened to you. You will find no one happy to welcome you, no one to prepare your dinner, and no one to get you to sleep. It is then that you remember the good life you had with your family. You will wish to have it, but you will not get it. And thus you will do your best to try to forget this wish."

Having camped for the night for a second day (which was as tough as the first day), they marched on and on in the desert for seven days—hungry, thirsty, and suffering from the blistering heat and sandstorms. That's right, they called the walking "marching," a new word in Tigrinya, which they had invented as a testimony to their exhausting experience. Soon they were close to the territory of the enemy. Their Italian commander, sitting on a horse in their midst, spoke to them in a loud voice. "O black Eritrean *ascari!* Those whom you are now going to fight against are but a bunch of shepherds. You may perhaps be frightened because they are whites. However, they are not like us. They do not possess guns, nor do they have ample bullets. They do not have binoculars like us, nor do they have mortars as we do. We alone are the brave whites; we, Italians, your masters. Hence, beat him (the enemy); do not be afraid of him. If we happen to find goats, camels, cattle, donkeys, or sheep, we will give you some to slaughter and eat. However, woe unto him who finds gold, silver, or any similar item and keeps it for himself. I shall flog his bare bottom with fifty-five lashes of the whip in front of everyone. Now then, have you heard?! I am the owner of all the spoils. I am your master; everything you find you hand it to me. You should feel gratified and privileged for fighting under the Italian banner. We, the Italian government, are great; we have ships, trains, guns, rifles, and airplanes. For this reason you should fight well for us." He finished by stating that they must all repeat as he shouted, "*Viva l'Italia; Viva Emanuele,* our king!"

This was what the young *Habesha* were told while preparing for war. All right, they were mercenaries. Weren't they? It would indeed be too much for them to expect to hear better words. When the commander was talking to them, however, he forgot that he was addressing the *Habesha,* who, unlike some other Africans who didn't have pride in their history and land, had a long history of resistance and, moreover, were endowed with honesty of heart and depth of mind. He forgot the *Habesha* soldiers were fighting because they sought bravery and heroism, not for the sake of a few pennies.

We know that a soldier preparing to fight will not fight bravely if he is not defending the safety and greatness of his country and that of his parents, wife, and children. Our Italian chief did not seem to have any of these notions. He treated his soldiers like one who has gathered children from an unknown place to do things for him. He would rebuke them, lie to them, and sometimes praise them. He treated them as if they were children, and he boasted to them about Italian bravery. Thus, when he finally told them to shout, "*Viva l'Italia!*," those who weren't thinking did so with a loud, melodious voice, while the wise ones, Tuquabo among them, got a lump in their throat and shed sad tears as they came to realize what was being told to them. The judicious *Habesha* soldiers felt ashamed when looking at the Bedouin shepherds, who were preparing to defend their country. The people of the desert were not particularly good at war. They lacked guns and were short of ammunition. They didn't have a king or a chief to lead them. Even so they did their best to save their land from aliens. On the other hand, it was strange to watch the *Habesha,* who at first did nothing when their land was taken and bowed to the Italians like dogs (as if that were not shameful enough indeed), preparing to fight those Arabs who wanted to defend their country. The *Habesha* were fighting for those who came to colonize and to make others tools of colonizing African neighbors, without anything of benefit to their country or society. There may be some who think that fighting the Arabs on behalf of the Italians and exterminating them from the face of the earth was forgivable considering that the Arabs and black Africans were historically enemies. But what was being done would one day lead to one's fall. If one day they come led by a Frenchman or an Italian to fight, didn't the *Habesha* know that the Arabs were going to pay back with vengeance? Don't they know that they would tell their children, generation after generation, that whatever they might forget, they should not forget the blood of *Habesha?* And that this bloodletting would go on forever?

As Tuquabo and the others marched in the direction of the Arab "enemy," the Arabs were preparing to fight the black mercenaries, the "Massawa slaves," as they called the conscripts. They were nomadic people, like the Tigre and Saho of our country, who traveled from one place to another, leading their livestock to green pastures to graze. Their livestock were donkeys, camel, goat, sheep, and horses. Their horses were famous for galloping like the wind without tiring, and were named "steel" for their strength. But it was the camel that was most beneficial to them. It carried all their goods, did not suffer much from thirst (it could go without drinking for a month), and carried his owner across the arid areas to any destination. The camel was reputed to have been blessed by the Prophet Mohammed. Since it was said that the Prophet blessed the animal, it was thus also kept for spiritual reasons. And that was why the Christians in our country did not keep the camel, but the Moslems did. A Christian who drank the milk of a camel was also considered to have converted to Islam. I remember one day when I was a small boy. I met a man leading camels, and I saw the man milking and drinking from a bowl. Being curious, I approached him and asked him if a camel's milk tasted good. "Sure," he said, and he offered me a taste. I sipped from his bowl, but when I started swallowing, I felt uncomfortable and spit it out. The man was not at all happy at my spitting out the holy milk, and he said "Aha," biting his lip. He would have taken out his wrath on me, had we been alone. The worst was to come later, though. When I reached home, as if doing a manly thing, I told my mother and a sister about the incident, and they were very upset with me. They hurled insults at me, shouted things like "You idiot! You fool! You good for nothing!" and so on. I asked them to explain to me why it was a sin or why they were so upset. As a Christian, of course, I had some knowledge of the Gospel, and I argued with them by citing biblical verses that said "Eat whatsoever is presented to you" and "It is what comes out of a mouth that makes a person unclean, not what goes into a mouth." My mother and sister did their best to bring counterexamples to defeat my argument. They told me that, of anything else, the worst thing that the *Habesha* returning from Arab hostage remembered of Arab wrongdoing to them was their being forced to drink camel milk. Much prayer and ritualistic cleansing by holy water was needed by those who drank the milk. So they told me, "You should think seriously who you are because you drank camel milk, without either being hungry or being forced." Because of their education, I knew that they could tolerate many things; but sensing my mother's grave concerns, I also realized that my mother could end up sending me for a two-week cleansing by the washing with holy water at the *Aba Meta'e* monastery or another blessed waterfall. So I told her that I actually had only tasted and not swallowed the camel milk. Relieved but also repenting, she said, "My dear son, I am sorry for getting angry at you" and kissed my forehead. We reconciled immediately.

All this story goes to show how much the milk of camel was feared by the *Habesha.* On the other hand, we did not know that it was their staple food in Tripoli. The desert Bedouins couldn't grow many crops, since there was not a single raindrop in the dry desert, in all seasons, summer or winter. I believe if they did not own animals, they would have perished. But God does not leave you with nothing. Where there is a small amount of water, they grow dates, which are also one of their favorite foods. They also make an intoxicating drink by extracting some liquid from the tree. But it is also said that if you were able to see an oasis, the area where water is abundant, you would ask yourself whether you are on earth or in heaven. These people live mostly around such areas, and that is where the traders also dwell.

The Arabs are the descendants of Ishmael, the son of Abraham's mistress, Hagar. Most of them are red in color, but the heat has darkened their skin slightly. They are beautiful, they tend to be tall. Their women were dressed like the women of our lowlands, and since they were always covered, they were lighter in complexion than their husbands. Their old men were graced by long beards. Their children were plump, nourished with milk. The men covered their bodies from head to toe. They wrapped turbans around their heads. They also wore cotton cloths on top. It was impossible to find an Arab or a Bedouin who traveled empty-handed. If they couldn't own a gun (which they adored most of all), they would have either a spear, or a sword, or a stick. The men who could afford it rode horses.

But for the Tigrinya the Arabs were notorious for bad behavior. They were untrustworthy, treacherous, and they held grudges. They had the reputation of being merciless killers if they got the occasion. According to the stereotype that was passed along by the Italians, to say that an Arab would respect a deal would be to lie. If you left trusting them because they made a vow, they would laugh at you. All this is what the white people said about them.

But they also had many good things to balance these bad behaviors. They were very diligent in upholding their religion. They never missed their prayers for any reason. Even if you were speaking with them, they would leave you to go and pray. No other society would have done this. They were also hospitable. But their best behavior was that they loved their freedom. They always counted on their God; they didn't mind whatever might happen.

The Arabs were even notorious for being careless when it came to working for their basic food needs, and this carelessness undoubtedly emanated from their so-called indolence. Again here were some stereotypical stories and slurs about them, which I copied from a book, in fact a book written in Italian. One story tells that there was a man whose wife was to deliver a baby. He went to a carpenter and gave money to quickly make a bed for the baby. The carpenter agreed and took the money. But when the man came back, there was no bed. He went back for the second and third time, but the bed was not made. The child was born, grew up, and reached age twenty. He married and told his father, "My wife is going to give birth, and I need a bed for the baby to sleep in." And the father replied, "Before you were born, I had paid a carpenter to make a bed for you. He may have finished it now. So go and fetch it from him." When he went to inquire about the bed his father had paid for, the carpenter angrily replied, "Why are you giving me such trouble, I don't like to do things in a hurry. And now, if you don't want me to make you a bed, here is your money, take it." He had failed to do a job given to him for twenty-one years. Another story has it that, in one home, a husband and his wife were sitting and drinking in the evening. The woman prepared a nice dinner. But she forgot to close the door and asked her husband to close it. He said, "Go close it yourself if you want to." They argued for a long time, telling each other, "Why don't you close it yourself?" The husband finally suggested to his wife, Fatima, that they should keep quiet and the first one to utter a word would close the door, and she agreed. While the food was in front of them, they kept quiet without moving a bit. Soon a beggar came. He begged, saying, "Wealth is a gift of Allah, and give me some alms from it." No one replied to him. Cursing how bad a family they were, he went inside and ate the food which God had kept for him until he was full. He ate the meat and hung the bones on the woman's neck. No one spoke while all this was happening. The beggar left with a full belly. Later a dog came around and entered the house when he saw the door open. With no one telling it to go, the dog was moving and sniffing around the house. It then came close to them. When it realized they were not speaking, trusting its instinct, it wanted to eat the bones hanging on the woman's neck. But the woman then chased the dog and shouted at it to go. Her husband then laughed and said, "You have spoken, go close the door." She agreed and went to close the door. They spent the night hungry and curled up, rubbing their bellies. In the morning, her husband mockingly said, "Mrs. Fatima, you shouldn't have entered into a bet with your better, I did not speak, but you did." "Yes, you are right, I spoke," she replied, "but if the dog had not come, I would not have said anything." In this way they spent the night hungry because they were too indolent to simply go and close the door.

Similarly, an old man went to collect prickly pears, but was overheated by the sun and prayed, telling himself that he would wait with his God until the sun cooled off. So he sat under shade. Then he saw a woman pass by while crying. He asked her why she was crying. She answered, "I cannot have a child. And my husband always beats me. He will not divorce me." The man told her that he would make sure she got a child, "as long as you pick my prickly pear." She agreed. When she went to pick for him, he took out his gun and removed some dirt from it using his knife. When she finished and came back, he said to her, "Take this and mix it with water and drink," and gave it to her. She drank the mix, and it proved to be not her antidote for birth, but her killer. Imagine where indolence takes them.

This is what was said about the character of Arabs. But seeing now how they were arming themselves to fight when told there was an alien army coming to attack them, no one can believe that supposed laziness after all. It was altogether a different proposition to see the very activities that were taking place. In the midst of the noisy sheep and goats, there were those who were preparing their armor, sharpening their swords, cleaning their guns, and sewing any torn material for their cavalry. In the chaos of war, one could see women wiping their tears while bringing food and weapons to their fighting men. One could witness children crying as their fathers prepared for war while the mothers wept. On the other hand, one could observe the Moslem Arab heroes vowing to fight the "infidels." Watching the elders encourage their sons, while the sheikhs facing Medina prayed to Mohammed to give them help and victory (with the whining of the anxious horses in the background), was an experience to which no person endowed with a human heart could stand indifferent.

After the preparation, it was time for departure. They kissed their children, parents, and relatives good-bye. Those who owned horses mounted them; those who didn't set out on foot. The brave ones were leading from the front and singing, "There is no God but God, and Mohammed is the Prophet." One of them stood and spoke to the Arab soldiers as follows: "Have a brave heart! Infidels coming to invade us is not a normal phenomenon; as it is said, the sons of Mohammed go to other places to rule and plunder, not others coming to rule and plunder them. We should not let something happen to us that did not happen to our fathers and grandfathers. We shouldn't shame ourselves. Either we liberate our land or we shall be buried there. We should take back to our people the sign of our victory, or let them hear of our death." He concluded by repeating, "Today is glory or doom." They felt buoyed up by his speech, and all were singing songs of war, louder and louder. Waving their swords, they vowed not to be mentioned as men if they didn't spill the blood of "those dogs." They were even murmuring to their horses that they were to have the blood of Christians for lunch. Encouraged by such inspirational messages, the Arab insurgents moved faster and faster, and, after traveling all night, they came to a watching distance from the Italian army of conscript soldiers. The Italian army commander blew the whistle for getting ready for the battle. He ordered all soldiers to be lined up in two lines, front and back, according to European military techniques. On the left and right flanks, the heavy artillery and machine-gun soldiers lined up. Having shown them their positions, he loudly ordered them to be "on guard." After that, he ordered them to attach their bayonets on to their guns, and then he told them to lie down on the ground. Not being culturally used to lying low in battle, the *Habesha* soldiers were confused by the order and wondered why they had to lie down instead of facing their enemy standing tall. They were, in fact, thinking that he was going to get them trampled by the horses. But in spite of this, they did what they were told.

Soon they were feeling anxious; they remembered their fathers and mothers, and they thought of their villages. They wondered who would bury them if they were to die here, with no one around to care for their graves. They understood how foolish it was to fight in a stranger's war with no benefit to one's country. They thought how frightening it would be even fighting in your land for your country when one single bullet could end your life—let alone fighting in alien lands for a foreign force. In such circumstances, there is no one, even the bravest, who would not tremble with fear. Well, in our country, fighting men are used to hiding their fear with boasting and agitating. But these conscripts weren't even able to do that! This is because these conscripts were trained in the Italian way, and the first thing they were told was to be quiet and still unless the commander orders otherwise. The Arabs felt different, deep in their hearts. They knew they were going to fight *for* their country *in* their country. If they were defeated, they knew where to run. If they were thirsty, they knew where to find water. If they sought shelter in a place, they would find someone to give them sanctuary. All these things boosted their morale. Moreover, since they were Moslems, they were also encouraged by what Mohammed had told them: that they would be rewarded in heaven to the extent that they killed Christians, and that they would go directly to heaven if they died in such a war. It seemed war was like a wedding for them. If they should ordinarily not have been as strict in following the rules of the Qur'an and somehow negligent of the teachings of Mohammed, on that day they were impatient to reap the blessings of heaven for themselves and their children; and, if they died as martyrs, to earn the rewards that can take them directly to "their *Jannah*," which is filled with honey, milk, and maidens. Yet, when they realized for a moment that death was really near, being mortal beings like all of us (how afraid we are of death, though we can't escape it sooner or later), they too hesitated.

Putting their faith in Mohammed, the Arab warriors went into battle with bravery and determination. But they entered the fight directly and went forward; they didn't have leaders who issued instructions. They looked like cattle thundering towards attacking hyenas. As they came forward kicking up dust, the Italian army conscripts (the *ascari*) poured bullets like water on them. Those in the frontline positions fell like leaves; some were directly struck by bullets; others came down together with their horses when the horses were hit. But the death of those in front did not deter the others. Running over the dead bodies of their brothers, the Arabs surged ahead, some falling and others running over the positions of the conscripts with the horses, which sprang like tigers. There, many a conscript who was lying down in the trenches was trampled by the horses, and others were slaughtered by sword-wielding men who were shouting, "*Jihad fi sefil Allah!*" At that moment, the Italian commander ordered the *ascari* to "stand up," although they did not wait until he ordered them.

Other Arab fighters were also penetrating from other sides. Anyone who observed the fighting from a distance would not have been able to tell from which direction the war had begun; he would not be able to identify where the Italian or Arab positions were. One could only see people moving and horses jumping. One could only see weapons flashing, guns firing, and dust clouding. And one could hear the screams of wounded fighters, the boasting of the killers, and the shrieking noise of horses. Our countrymen were finding it difficult to fight with the sword, as it was not that common in their land. But when they saw that it wasn't getting better, they took out their swords and started slaughtering. The bent sword of the *Habesha* could chop two or three men at the same time. Since it could bring down many men at once, the Arabs panicked and started stepping back slowly. The *Habesha* warriors were pressing while the Arabs continued retreating, after which they turned and started running away when the onslaught became too much to bear. But, let truth be told, there was no one who could run faster than the Ethiopians, and they caught and killed many of those unlucky Arabs. It was a horrible and strangely bewildering moment to watch the Arabs running, the *Habesha* chasing, the Italians shouting—all three different cultures, with different fighting styles, mixed up in the war. For the *Habesha* fighting a war was to push forward, whatever the cost; for the Italians it was to abide by the order of your commander, even if an enemy comes face to face, for nobody should move unless commanded (as they say). And above all, nobody should shoot unless under instructions. They tell you to do nothing, even if you are slaughtered, until they give their order! For the Arabs, first you should run fast towards your enemy, and then, if things turn out bad, you run for your life. In short, the *Habesha* work with incomparable strength, the Italians through arrangement, and the Arabs through action and risk. But to tell the truth, nobody could outstrip the *Habesha* in running, and when the Arabs fell to their hands (how pitiful), they were murdering like blood-drunk tigers, while everywhere else the two groups ran after each other like hunting dogs and escaping gazelles. At times the retreating Arabs stood back and killed a pursuing *Habesha* before themselves dying an inescapable death, but determined to die in a manner by which they could go to *Jannah,* which is abundant with milk and honey, as Mohammed had promised them. In addition to this, the Arabs had another tactic, which was to lie in ambush and do the killing there. In this way they slaughtered many sons of the *Habesha.* In the end, those who had horses fled to safety and those who didn't were either killed or captured. And so it ended with full victory for the *Habesha.* No, I am wrong. It was for the Italians.

Late that night, the Italians had the *ascari* set up the camp and light fires, and let them eat their dinner of meat from the goats they looted. The *ascari* filled their stomachs with meat and felt satisfied. They were very tired and fell asleep where they were immediately after dinner. Tuquabo was one of those who stood out as a war hero on that day. He was praised for his deeds by his peers. While preparing for sleep, however, he was called to be one of the night guards. Having been in battle the whole day, he was upset by the call and said to himself, "Alas, this is like going to a bad wife after spending the day with a bad ox. After sweating all day, do I deserve to stay up through a sleepless night!?" Even so, as a soldier he knew that he wouldn't be severed from his duty because he pleaded or his commanders felt sympathetic with him, and therefore he swallowed his pain and went for duty. To be a night guard meant that you had to sit in a place where you could observe people coming in and going out, and you must be cautious and alert in case an enemy came by unexpectedly. To be a night guard also meant that you shouldn't be found talking with another, or just sitting, or sleeping. That would result, without any hesitation, in your being shot by your commanders instantly. The night guard must stay alert and stand still for two hours, whether it was hot or cold outside. Whatever happened, he was not supposed to move from his place or move around. This job was exhausting and of great concern for the conscripts, and their lament was expressed in the refrain they sang: "Libya, Libya, Libya, running during daytime, and guarding at night."

Tuquabo went out as a night guard with some of his comrades. They took turns in their positions. When his turn came in the late night, Tuquabo took up his gun, wore his ammunition belt, and stood at the guard post. Because it was bitterly cold, he covered himself with a blanket. The place was so quiet; neither the sounds of wild beasts nor the screeching sound of a cricket were heard. In our country, one never feels lonely; even if it's scary to hear sounds of wild animals at night, listening to them eases your heart nonetheless. You feel there is something around you. Here, Tuquabo was standing alone like a chunk of wood. He only saw a vast area of empty land surrounding him on all sides. In the moment he remembered his homeland and said to himself, "What would my parents be doing now? Maybe they are crying when they look at my unoccupied bed? And I am here alone in this desert in gloom. What a land is this? No single tree, no grass you could step on, no twinkles of light (or signs of cooking fire) to be seen from a distant village, no sound of animals. Everywhere you go is filled with sand, day or night, endless sand. And this they call a country! Ehmm. The Arabs fight for this barren land. And us? A curse be upon us! We didn't do anything when the Italians came to take our fertile land. Not only that, we led the Italians like the blind and carried them like children and allowed them to enter our homeland, and now we are supporting them to conquer this land. We let our country be taken, and we are now instruments to occupy someone else's country. We lost our country, and we are extending our hands to colonize other lands. How would the Arabs be fighting if they had as good a land as ours? When you think of it, the Arabs here are nomads, and they shouldn't have cared too much, as they could have moved easily, leaving this barren land to the Italians. But despite all this, they did not kneel down to Italian rule!"

Tuquabo further roamed with his thoughts. "Back home, this time I'd be a long time asleep and awake. If there was a party, I would be drumming with my friends, and there would be girls and boys singing together with the intensity of the music. We would sing away the night with many sweet songs like 'Have faith in God and nothing will happen to you' and 'Honey, would you like a drink in a glass cup?' Also we would horse around, or sometimes wrestle so hard that we would throw each other high up to the sky before falling on the ground. This particular wrestling was called 'the wrestling of the monks of Debre-Bizen Monastery,' because the monastery was hidden so high at the top of a mountain that it seemed to touch the stars. If you did the trick of the 'Debre-Bizen Monastery' and threw off your opponent when wrestling, you surely showed him the stars! There was a wrestler called Haile who was so good that he was nicknamed Satan. Another, called Tewolde, was also very good. In the midst of this, one would hear the hyenas laughing, the dogs barking, and see the moon brightly lit as the shimmering stars surrounded her. Your heart melted. After the wrestling you would drink your milk and be lulled to sleep on the soft grass."

When he mentioned sleep, Tuquabo remembered where he was. He woke up from his thoughts as one would wake up from sleep, and he looked around to find himself standing alone in the desert. As the tears accumulated, time seemed eternal. All of a sudden, Tuquabo found himself singing. "You are drying up in the empty field, thrown in a place you know not, neither for your father's nor your mother's sake." He was surprised when he realized he was singing in the utmost silence, and he kept quiet. A while later, the next night shift guard came to replace him and, as they exchanged identification code words, Tuquabo said, "You took your time, eh?" to which the comrade replied, "You thought so, but the time is just now." Tuquabo was a kind person and knew that staying all alone as a night guard was quite stressful; he therefore went to see the officer to ask if he could accompany his comrade in the night job. Moved by the thought, the officer told him to do whatever he wished. As Tuquabo went back to accompany his *Habesha* comrade, he cried lamenting that the *Habesha* with all their heroic deeds and love among themselves would have been useful if all they did was for their land, not for the benefit of strangers for whom they worked as mercenaries in a strange land. The two were there left alone for the rest of the night, and they chatted until morning. Befriended this way, Tuquabo and his companion marched together from place to place, as fellow soldiers. Beaten by the heat, the sun and dust, and without water, they trekked in the wilderness for days and days on end.

FOUR

The Thirst of Death

Early one morning the general commander passed the order that everyone should pack to leave and shouted, "Gird up your loins and move!" For himself, he carried water on his mule. So did his Italian companions. But who would look out for the conscripts? Even if they dried up from thirst, who would really care? They marched anyway. Without knowing where they were heading, they slugged along and couldn't find any water on their way. Not a trace of water. If you asked where the commanding officer was, he would be in his tent safekeeping his water. He had guards around his tent and stayed silent inside. A proverbial saying goes, "There are times when fighting a war is easier than resisting hunger." Pity the conscripts who were on the brink of death from thirst yet were guarding the tent for somebody who carried water. Nobody could understand how terrible it must have felt for those who needed to get a share of the water. They were like the rich man in hell who longed for a drop of water from Lazarus. They would have loved to get a taste of water from anyone. But they weren't there to privilege themselves by quenching themselves with water; they were supposed to stand there and prevent any other conscript from coming close to the tent. Whenever they heard the splash of water, their hearts would jump. It was exactly like watching a dog whose eyes, while one is eating, are raised and lowered following the movement of one's hand. They were, after all, like dogs, if you compared them with the Italians. In fact, dogs fared better; they at least ate their masters' leftovers.

Nobody knew what those conscripts who were abandoned outside, who looked like monkeys hampered from drinking water, were doing. Some of them were restlessly moving back and forth; some lay down throbbing. Others were desperately digging up the sand by hand in case they could find water. Poor souls, they thought they could dig up water easily in the same way as in their homeland. They found the sand hotter as they dug deeper, and losing all their patience, they looked up to the sky and prayed to their God in despair, "O All-Seeing God, we are in distress." A few among them (not only one or two) had patience and would try to calm down the rest but were out of words. How would it be possible to utter a word when the throat was dry and the tongue couldn't get any saliva? Their lips were chapped and dry, their eyes dull, their faces ashy, and their eyelids covered with dust. They hoped for wet night breezes to come at night, but there was no breeze or fog in that wilderness. Even if wetness had fallen, without grass or trees, the hot sands would have soaked it all. So they spent the night roasted by the heat.

The order to move was given again the next morning, and the soldiers walked slowly. The sun was unbearably hot, the sand got hotter, and dust blew up. Many felt their hearts sinking, and order lost its meaning. They were dropping their guns and ammunition, and staggered. By midday, many had spinning heads and fell down and curled up and remained there, dark blood flowing out of their noses. And the remaining blood was forced out with the last energy of their dying bodies. Some couldn't continue marching at all and collapsed where they were to become food for the vultures. When he saw this, the Italian commander-in-chief disappeared on his mule, leaving them behind. He was afraid that they might kill him, but in fact nobody dared. Let truth be told, would a *Habesha* dare revolt against an Italian? It was very unlikely. But for the Italian, the *Habesha* was like a weak donkey, which you couldn't kill for meat or hide and therefore would leave behind to die in the field under God's hand. The cowardly Italian, who gained his pride and fame from the strong young *Habesha,* thus escaped when he knew that they were weakened and dying of thirst. But for him, they were just mercenaries; they had been bought anyway.

Gradually the entire army of the conscripts was in disarray. Groups started dispersing in all directions without knowing where to go. Tuquabo's group luckily headed on a route which happened to take them to a place where they chanced upon a well. They crowded up to drink, but it turned out the water was deep. Using a rope, a few of them then began to descend deep down to the bottom of the well to reach the water. Once there, they were chewing mud and sending up capfuls of it to the comrades on top, in order to help quench the thirst. As the comrades on top waited expectantly, those who were beneath inside the well suddenly discovered a hidden wellspring, whose opening was sealed off by a layered chunk of cloth, but was gushing with water the instant they removed the covering. All drank and washed, helping each other. A few of the conscript leaders who had mules also gave water to their beasts. They were the few blessed, lucky ones.

About one-fourth of them, in numbers. Even if it had taken them three days of trekking to find the water. As for the other wandering units of conscripts, some fell into enemy hands, while the corpses of others lay everywhere. A few of them had also, indeed, the luck to reach a well with water, but they stampeded it like a mob, like buzzing flies that fall into a bowl of milk, and they died by falling on top of one another. Those who were trampled under were suffocating, and tried to make it up by stabbing with knives the bodies of the comrades who were falling on them. With their entrails soaked in blood, they all perished together there, with bellies open of both the killers and the killed. Oh, it was a horrible sight. You wouldn't even wish that to happen to your enemy. May the parents of these sons of *Habesha* not see this; may anyone who has a human heart not see this. This had become the end of the brave young Ethiopians. And the Italian who led them to this and made this happen was going to have a good night's sleep in his homeland. Nothing was going to happen to him. Everything worked well for him.

The cruelty of it! And what happened to those conscripts who got away from this hell? They still had to fight their way out, and the Arabs started killing them one by one. The griot sang, "One by one they got fewer" when he mourned the death of Negusse, the legendary *Habesha* war hero. It is true that the *Habesha* people were brave, but unfortunately the Arabs were coming in numbers. In the end, the Arabs drove them out to the rim of the sea, and the surviving conscripts eventually embarked on the ship that took them off towards their home. On their return journey, they were grieving their comrades who fell in battle and died, and mournfully sang, "Let no one go to Tripoli, lest they be cut with long knife and sword."

The parents, brothers, and sisters were, of course, wondering about what happened to the conscripts during all those days of war in "Tripoli." They always were in fear and tears, preoccupied day and night by the thought of their sons in the war, as they waited for their return. Those parents who had other children at home were at least feeling somehow consoled by their presence. It was sad to see those like the parents of Tuquabo, whose only son was born to a family through a lot of prayers and promises, and who was gone to a foreign land to risk his life in the service of strangers, leaving behind his aging parents. There is a truth to the proverbial saying that "the heart of youth is swollen with pride." It is distressing to think that one could leave those parents who only want your love, who only want the best for you, who pray for your safety and who want to see themselves die before you, and instead go to serve those strangers who do not see you as any better than a dog. It would have been good if you'd go for trade or out to the field to hunt game or for something harmless of that order. But no, going to war, to a land of thirst and famine, death, and degradation, is simply incomprehensible. This is not just one story, but the story of many parents, but since we are talking about Tuquabo's parents, let's go back to them.

It is easier to think about them than to try to put in words how the time seemed so long for Tuquabo's parents during those two years. It was pitiful to see how saddened they were and how their health was deteriorating in the last days of their life, as a result of his absence. Each night, before they went to bed, they pleaded, singing *Kyrie Eleison,* and prayed, "O Lord, please let the only son you gave us return home safely. Don't let us die before our eyes see him once again." His mother was having nightmares and was calling her son's name in her sleep. There were times when the dream would seem so true that she believed she had met Tuquabo in real life, and she would stretch out her arms to hug him, before suddenly waking from her slumber. Once awake, she could never fall back to sleep, and muttered in pain throughout the night. Everything reminded her of her son. Whenever she saw a young lad passing by, she thought how wonderful it would be to see Tuquabo there walk like that. If she heard mothers talk about their sons, her heart went out to him, to the one who was overseas. If she heard her cows mooing, she felt miserable from the thought that the heir-owner was absent, and she would think lamentably about the futility of milking them or making ghee of their milk, for it would be for others to eat and drink, as Tuquabo was gone. "Oh, Tuquabo! Tuquabo," she would cry, and go on agonizing, "What good is a harvest if there is no one to eat? If it isn't for my son Tuquabo, what's it for me, but to add to my grief?" Such outbursts were becoming her only conversation with her only son. The neighbors were sorry for her to see her in this condition, and they prayed in their hearts that God would help her by returning her son. Her husband was worried for his wife's mental health. For indeed she was sometimes spending the whole day calling her son's name, like a person who has gone insane.

A letter had once arrived at the house from Tuquabo. She grabbed it and almost wanted to swallow the paper, kissing it over and over, pressing it to her face, and holding it close to her heart. And when, another time, Tuquabo sent a photograph of himself, she was speechless and didn't know what to do with it, as she had never seen a picture before.

It had all seemed to her like a dream. She never parted with the photo; and she loved to show her friends her son's picture, feeling happy and proud to talk about him at length. Time went by, and a rumor went around one day that the conscripts were coming home. The news was like a strong wind that stirs up the embers of a dying fire, before finally blowing out the flame with its massive force. It was like that for Tuquabo's mother. It gave life briefly to her weary heart, but then her heart, pounding with joy and excitement (and she was of old age), made an artery rupture and stopped beating altogether. In a blink of a moment, she passed away thus, calling her son's name. Her husband fell into the deepest sorrow imaginable. Besides missing his son, he had also lost his wife. He remained alone in the empty space at home. Life was hard for the old man, who in the remaining years of his life most needed dignity and love but instead was deprived of his child and spouse. It would be different for a young person, who could be deceived and encouraged by worldly life, which is hard to do for one who is old enough to know the vanity of the world. How could he be consoled? One would think that the news of the returning conscripts should have rekindled some hope in Tuquabo's father, but he, too, was overwhelmed by the events unfolding. When he first heard the news, he was tormented by the uncertainty of not knowing whether his son was dead or among the survivors of the war. And who could tell? As they say, "If there is water, there is winter," which worried him. Who could vouch that Tuquabo would survive the unknown and endless hazards of the journey at sea, on his way back home? And even if Tuquabo came back safely, it was perturbing to think of having to tell him of the death of his mother. Tuquabo's father couldn't eat, drink, or sleep. He stopped talking to people. He spent his days at home, sobbing in misery—alone. The neighbors were kind enough to come and visit him once in a while and ask him, "What would you like us to bring you to eat and drink?" But it is hard to deal with a person who resents himself, and it was getting harder for him to find solace. So he preferred to be left alone, and spent his days contemplating his misery. Only his flesh was in this world; his heart was in a different world now, thinking about his wife and son. In fact, he was growing forgetful; he wouldn't know where he was. And with the loss of his mind's eye, he had no use for his sight and hearing.

After some time, word was heard that the conscripts had reached the port of Massawa. Indeed, the conscripts had made it to Massawa. After two years, the fortunate ones arrived in Massawa, to return to their homes. But no one could know the thoughts that filled their heads. They were now in the land that they had badly missed. They saw the great mountain chains, which were the topic of their daily conversations and night dreams, and they couldn't resist their tears. The landscape was part of their hearts and souls. It was impossible to forget the land, even when left behind in peace and prosperity, let alone when left in adversity. They were struck by a tremendous feeling of joy and longing when they saw in Massawa the brown people like them carrying loads, and they were bursting with a mix of laughter and crying at the same time. One can only imagine how they would react when they reached Asmara, if they felt such euphoria on entering Massawa, where for most of them there were no families and relatives to meet.

When they heard that the conscripts were entering Asmara, many people from the villages—children, women, old and young—gathered in the city. Some had traveled on foot, others on mules. Those who did not know whether their loved ones were among the returning waited in fear and hope. Fear, because they wouldn't know if the loved one was dead; hope, for their safe return. Not knowing the train hours, the villagers were going back and forth to the station to ask about the train's arrival. It was heartrending to watch the *Habesha* agents in authority there, who were proudly shouting "Pronto" answering the phone in Italian, but who either simply ignored or disdainfully looked down on their inquiring country fellows. It could be worse. Occasionally, there would be whipping, beating, and shoving. It was then also to mark moments such as this that the people sang, "God save us from your wrath, the *Habesha* clerk has turned against his own."

The train finally arrived in Asmara with the conscripts. A huge crowd of people gathered at the station as it arrived. Those who didn't know of its arrival rushed to the station from home or work, carrying food and drinks. Having fenced off the station, the guards, who were armed with long whips, and with pistols hanging on their left hips, stood there smugly as if ready to block the way to a big party. Their job was to whip away any *Habesha* who came closer. No mistake about that; that was their task, their order. Only the *Habesha* were whipped and chased away. They wouldn't dare to touch anyone who was from overseas. Yes, it was again the *Habesha* who was the dupe.

As the train entered the station whistling, the conscripts waved the scarves in their hands. Some women ululated, others were crying. "The train comes smoking and your mother's daughter is crying," sang the women. The crowd pushed forward, which led to a commotion, after which the guards started beating and whipping anyone in their way. When, after a while, the conscripts came out lined up on one side of the train, they were flooded by the crowd. The crowd seemed like growling sheep or goats which ran about to fetch their little ones, bucking and hitting anything on their way, while the little lambs moaned and jumped to find their mothers. There was noise, chaos, tears, and calling out of names on all sides as people fought to find their loved ones. While those reunited were hugging and kissing, others jostled through in a desperate search for their loved ones.

In the end, when the people who found their loved ones separated from the crowd, the chaos settled down. But not really. The people whose relatives had died, but nonetheless had decided to come to the station to find out for themselves from the comrades within the battalion, started to scream and cry in grief. They were inconsolable. Their loss was the more painful because also they were unable to claim the remains of their sons and loved ones. Not knowing whether the bodies were eaten by fish in the sea or by vultures and hyenas in the desert drove their grief beyond imagination.

The memory of the "Cetimo" battle was particularly agonizing. In this regard, I remember the story of an Ethiopian woman who had lost her brother. She had left her homeland with her brother and had come to Asmara. I think they were only two of them. Then her brother joined the conscripts and died in the war. She had learnt about it a long time ago. She was shrouded in grief from top to toe. Hair shaven, eyes hollow from crying, cheeks drooped by tears, skin scratched and torn in distress, she came to the station in a tattered black dress—which was all she had left to show as a legacy to her brother. She had been sobbing silently when the train pulled in, and after the conscripts got off, she started calling her brother's name. When everybody started leaving the station with their loved ones, and she knew definitely she had lost her brother, she burst into tears and loud screams. It was heartbreaking to see. Swept by grief and rocking like a person with a severe stomach pain, she was moaning and groaning in distress. "What would my people say to me, think of me? Oh brother, we left our homeland together—am I destined to return alone? If they asked me where he fell, I wouldn't be able to tell. If they asked me where he was buried, I wouldn't ever know where he was. What would they say to me? I left my home country with nobody to support me except you my brother. Now I don't know where to go. Tell me what to do . . ." As she muttered those words, her feminine shriek and cry pierced the hearts of the people like a blade. That shriek could move even those with a heart of stone. On the other hand, what people saw that day was not extraordinary. It continued to happen each time conscripts arrived in the train station.

After the bedlam, everyone went home. Tuquabo's father had waited in his village because he was bedridden by that time. Tuquabo therefore went directly to visit his father. When they met they were in each other's arms for a long, long time. It is rather easier to imagine than to put in words how they were feeling toward each other at that time, for it is difficult to express love in words. Tuquabo asked about his mother. Trying to find excuses, the father said, "She is visiting somewhere and she would be coming tomorrow . . ." But Tuquabo's heart could not rest. Deep inside, he knew and told himself that if his mother were alive, she would have waited for him, knowing that the conscripts were returning that day. His tears were falling, and soon Tuquabo and his father were sobbing violently. His father finally told him of his mother's death. Learning that she died right before his arrival put him in greater sorrow. And with feelings of regret and with a cramp in his stomach from grief, he wailed the following dirge for her.

Going to a distant land,
Not for the honor of my homeland
Leaving my family behind,
In agony and tears, for two years
And knowing I killed my mother, to follow my vanity
Here I return dragging my feet
To show my unworthiness
To those I upset, my people and beloved ones.
I deserve their curse

Lacking nothing, I had plenty to eat, drink
And clothing to cover
But left my homeland, oh, such rashness
Here I return to show my unworthiness.
Let all who can speak,
Mouth their condemnation

I was one blessed by his grace and with riches
Why did I put myself through this?
Mother, I know it's because of me
My sweet mother, I have failed you,
Deep within the devil deceived me.
So be it, I accept your curse
To be denied of an eye, tooth, and hand
And be barren like a fiend
I deserve worse;
So be it, let all fall upon me.

Farewell to arms
I am done with Italy and its tribulations
That robbed me off my land and parents
I am done with conscription and Italian medals
Farewell to arms!

Some days later, Tuquabo asked to be discharged from the Italian Army and returned to his village. His father didn't live much longer, and the death of his mother continued to be the most painful experience for him for a long time to come.

* * *

Gebreyesus Hailu (1906–1993) was a prominent and influential figure in the cultural and intellectual life of Eritrea during the Italian colonial period and in the post-Italian era in Africa. With a PhD in theology, he was vicar general of the Catholic Church in Eritrea and played several important roles in the Ethiopian government, including that of cultural attaché at the Ethiopian Embassy in Rome, member of the national academy of language, and advisor to the Ministry of Information of the Ethiopian government. Hailu's novel, *The Conscript,* written in 1927, is based on a true story of Eritrean soldiers conscripted by the Italian colonial army to fight in Libya, whom Hailu met on his way to study in Italy.

Ghirmai Negash, translator of *The Conscript,* is a professor of English and African literature at Ohio University. He is the author of *A History of Tigrinya Literature in Eritrea* and coeditor of *Who Needs a Story?* His recent publications include articles and essays on Eritrean and South African literatures.

Laura Chrisman, author of the introduction to this English translation, is a professor of English at the University of Washington, where she holds the Nancy K. Ketcham Endowed Chair. She is the author or editor of several books, including, as coeditor, *Colonial Discourse and Post-Colonial Theory: A Reader.*